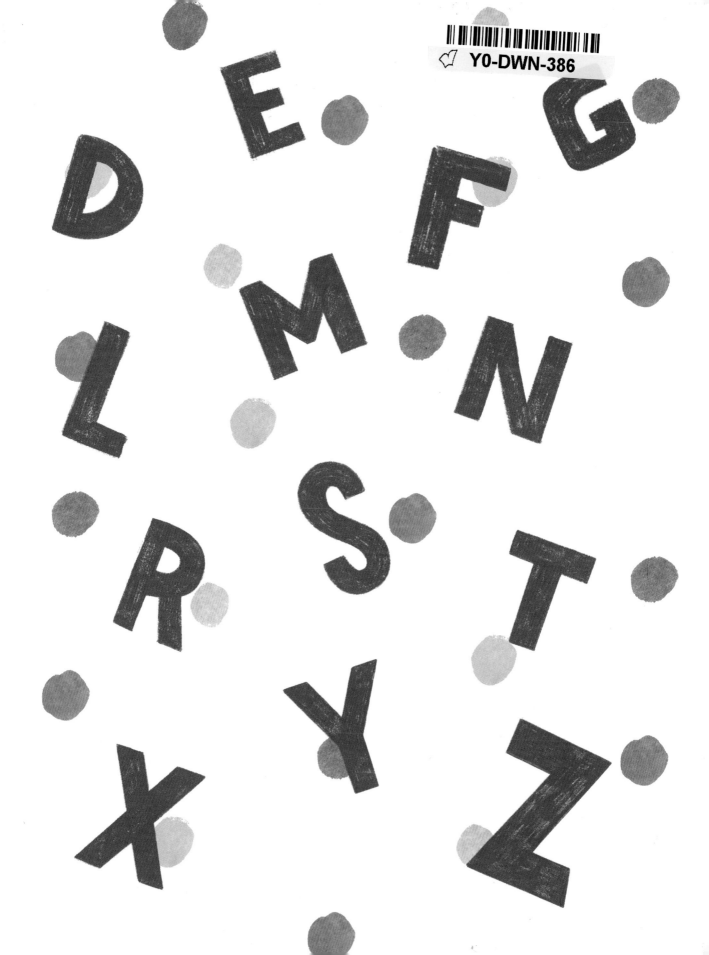

For Amara and Leela, for having the courage to be true to yourselves.

—MH

To my mom, for always encouraging me to reach high, go far, and be a little wild.

—MV

ABOUT THIS BOOK

The illustrations for this book were done digitally with some acrylic on Bristol texture collages. This book was edited by Farrin Jacobs and designed by Neil Swaab with art direction from Saho Fujii. The production was supervised by Kimberly Stella, and the production editor was Jen Graham. The text was set in Alice, and the display type was hand-lettered.

A is for AMBITIOUS

By MEENA HARRIS

Illustrated by MARISSA VALDEZ

LB
LITTLE, BROWN AND COMPANY
New York Boston

BOSS

AMBITIOUS!

LOUD

TIOUS!

INTENSE!

LOUD!

EMOTIONAL!

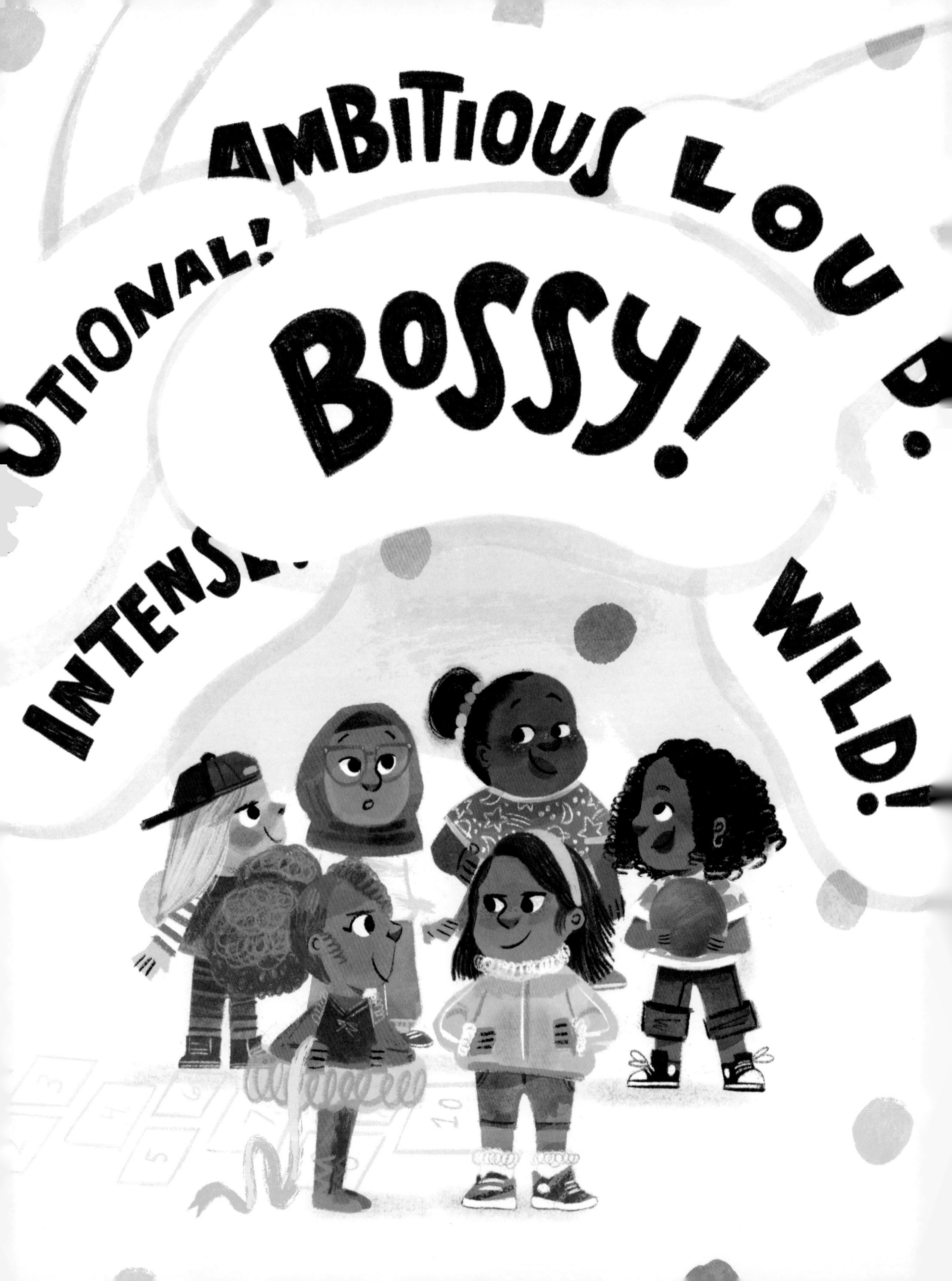

AMBITIOUS
LOUD
OTIONAL!
BOSSY!
INTENSE
WILD!

I have big ideas, hopes, and wishes.

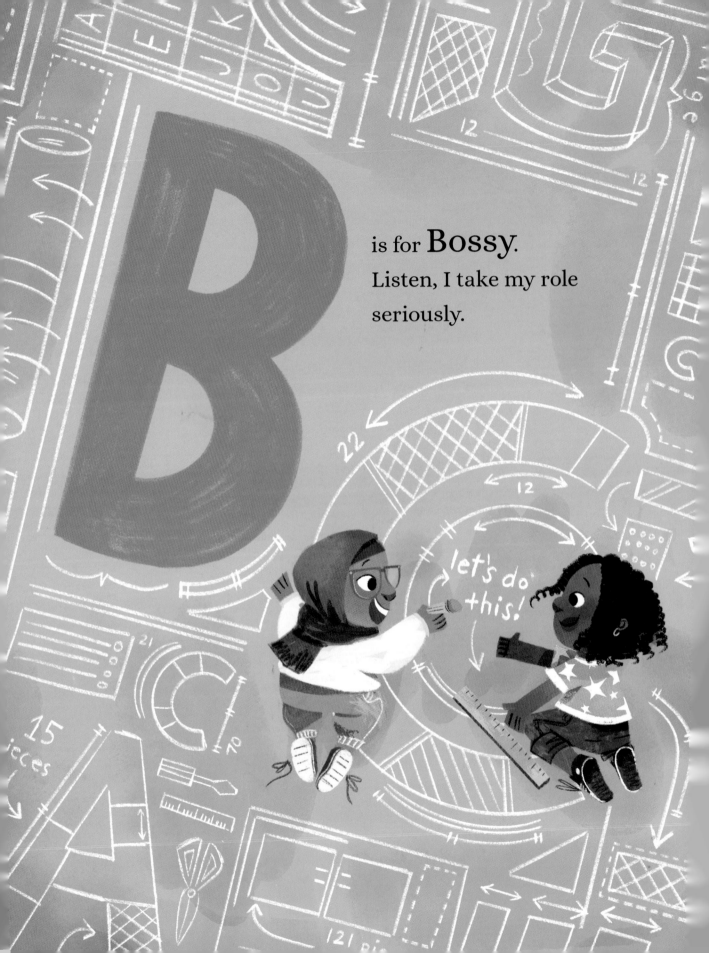

is for **Bossy**.
Listen, I take my role
seriously.

is for **Confident**.

Someday I could have my own monument!

D is for
Determined.

When we put our minds
together, everyone wins.

is for **Emotional**.

My feelings are valid; my heart is full.

is for **Feminist**,
a great thing for anyone to be—
if you believe in equity.

is for **Go-getter.**
Let's chase our dreams and
make the world better.

is for when I'm feeling **Headstrong**.
I'm not afraid to speak up if something is wrong.

is for **Intense**.
I like to concentrate so everything makes sense.

is for **Judgy**.

My beliefs are informed—I don't
share them without studying.

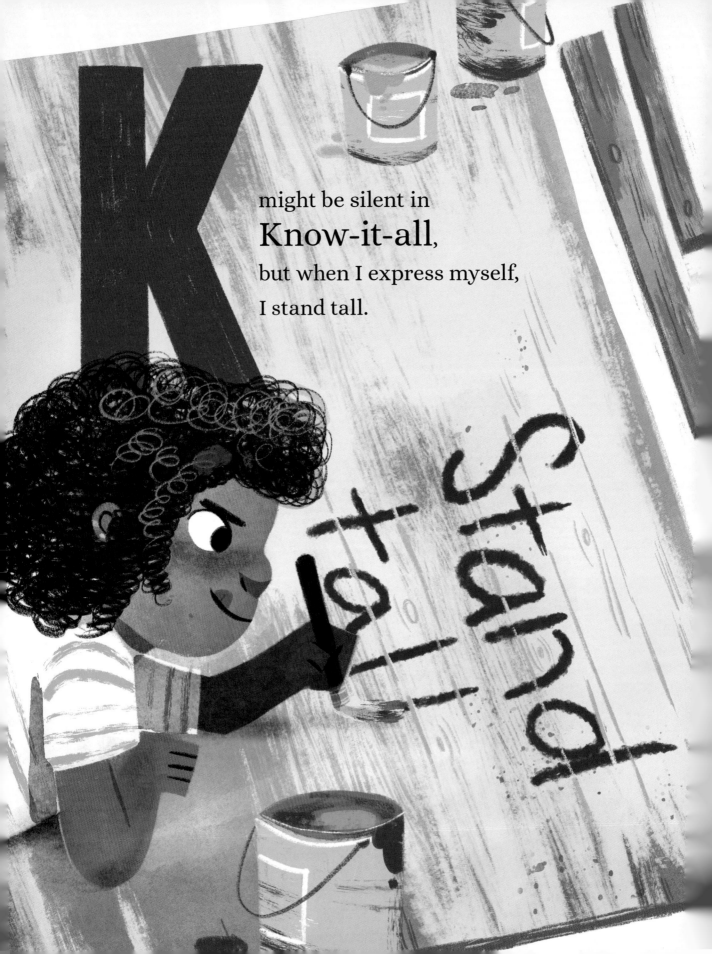

K

might be silent in
Know-it-all,
but when I express myself,
I stand tall.

L is for when my voice is Loud.
I want to be heard—I'm passionate
and proud.

is for too **Much**.

I am *so* many things. I have a special touch.

N is for **NO**. Because setting boundaries helps me grow.

is for **Opinionated**. Keeping every thought to yourself is *so* overrated!

P is for **Persistent**.
I won't give up. I *always* go the distance!

Q is for **Quirky**.
I am unique and special—only *I* can be *me*!

is for **Relentless**.

I have goals, I have plans, I will settle for nothing less.

is for **Sensitive**.

I'm compassionate, I have a lot to give.

T is for Trouble.
Good trouble, to be exact.
I won't shy away from the struggle,
and that's a matter of fact.

U

U is for **Unyielding**.
I'm on a mission; I'll keep building.

V

is for **Vulnerable**, when I want to be seen,
or the private moments in between.

W

well, that's for **Wild**.
I am free—my imagination is unbridled.

ROBOTICS LAB

X

is for all the things I haven't learned just yet
and all the versions of me I still haven't met.

Y

is for **Young**.

I bring a fresh perspective while honoring heroes unsung.

is for the **Zillions** of girls,
everywhere, all around the world.

We are more than one thing.
We'll be seen *and* heard.
We are all the letters in the alphabet.
And every last word.